The Secret Mermaid

Reef Rescue

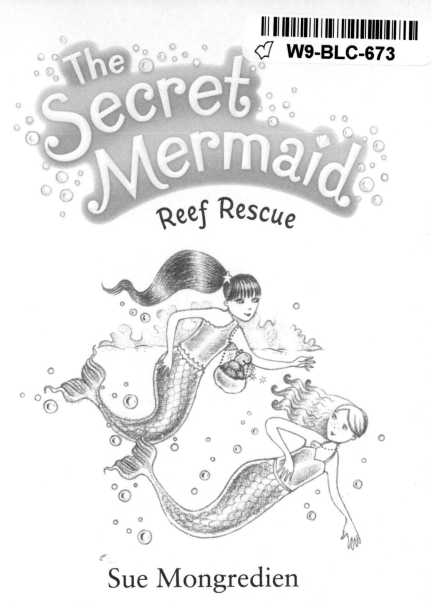

Sue Mongredien

Illustrated by Maria Pearson

USBORNE

For Bea Hanney, with lots of love

First published in the UK in 2009 by Usborne Publishing Ltd., Usborne House,
83-85 Saffron Hill, London EC1N 8RT, England. www.usborne.com

This edition published in America in 2016 AE.
PB ISBN 9780794536862   ALB ISBN 9781601304087
JFMA   JJASOND/16   01527-5
Printed in China

Contents

The Mermaids of the

Molly

Ella

Delphi

Shivana

Undersea Kingdom

Coral

Queen Luna

Princess Silva

Pearl

Chapter One

"We're back!" Molly Holmes called through the open front door. She wiped the sand off her bare feet on the doormat, steadying herself against the white cottage wall. Her parents were a little way behind on the path up from the beach, pushing her baby brother Toby in his stroller, which also held an assortment of buckets, shovels and fishing nets. Molly smiled at the thought of the new shells in her pocket.

She had quite a collection now – long, blue
mussel shells, fan-shaped scallop shells, and
some curving, rounded
shells with holes in
them, that her dad
reckoned had
once been home
to hermit
crabs. Of all
the shells she
had though,
not one of them
was as special as
the piece of conch
shell that Gran had
given her when they'd
moved into The Boathouse – for Molly had
discovered that *that* particular shell was full of
mermaid magic!

Molly dusted off the last grains of sand. "Gran? Are you there?" she called, walking into the front room.

It seemed gloomy inside after the bright light of the sun, and it took Molly's eyes a moment to adjust. Gran was on the sofa with her feet up on a stool and her eyes closed.

Molly padded in quietly and sat at the table, picking up her seaside spotter book, which she'd left there this morning. Her parents had bought it for her when they'd told her they'd all be moving to the seaside, and it was full of things to look out for on the beach

 – easy things like limpets and seagulls, but some trickier things too, like blennies and sandworms.

Today she'd seen a jellyfish washed up on the sand – she'd almost stepped on it, until she'd spotted it there at the last moment, round and still, edged with a purple rim. She flipped through the pages until she saw a picture of one just like it – a moon jellyfish, it was called – and checked the box next to it.

She leafed through the book while she waited for her parents. At the very back, there was a section on coral reefs, and she gazed at the colorful images in delight.

Even the names of the fish sounded exciting –
she couldn't resist reading them out.
"Clownfish, pufferfish, zebra fish, parrotfish,
sea stars…"

"Scorpionfish, sea snakes…" a voice
chimed in.

Molly turned around to see Gran smiling at her.
"Oops, sorry," she said. "Did I wake you up?"

"I was only resting my eyes," Gran said.

"I was just looking at these creatures from
the coral reef," Molly explained, going over to
show her the pictures. "They're so amazing!"

Gran nodded. "They are," she said. "It's
another world – like a rainforest under the sea.
And it's home to thousands of creatures…well,
until recently, anyway." She sighed. "I heard on
the radio that large areas of the reef have
become damaged and bleached lately, which is
when the corals become ill and lose their color.

Our ocean reefs are in great danger of dying."

"Dying?" Molly echoed in dismay. Her thoughts turned immediately to her mermaid friends who lived at the bottom of the ocean, and she wondered what was happening there. A mermaid named Coral looked after the reefs with the help of her own magical conch piece, but ever since Carlotta, the Dark Queen of the ocean, had stolen this shell fragment – and four others like it – Molly knew that Coral had been powerless to protect her area.

If only they could find Coral's piece of the shell and help make the reefs healthy again! Molly glanced across at Gran, wishing she could discuss it with her, but she knew she mustn't. Even though Gran had once been a secret mermaid herself, just like Molly was now, Molly had been sworn to secrecy by the Merqueen about her amazing mermaid adventures.

In came her parents at that moment, making a noisy clatter with the buckets and shovels. Toby let out a shout of excitement when he saw Molly and Gran, and waved his fat little arms.

Gran beamed and got up slowly to fuss over him.

"All right, who's hungry?" Mrs. Holmes asked. "Molls, will you come and give me a hand making supper, please?"

Molly got up obediently, but her mind was full of the images from the coral reef page of her book.

Oh, please let my shell work its magic tonight so that I can visit the mermaids again, she thought to herself, as she began washing lettuce leaves at the sink. *I can't bear the thought of the beautiful reefs dying!*

Later that evening, Molly was in her pajamas with her teeth brushed in record time. "I've never known you be so eager to go to bed," her dad laughed as he came into her bedroom to shut the curtains. "Has all that sea air worn you out?"

"It must have," Molly replied innocently, although she couldn't quite look him in the eye. She busied herself arranging her conch-shell necklace on the bedside table, then sat up to see her gran's twinkling gaze upon her.

Her parents and gran said goodnight, then left Molly alone in her bedroom. Even with the curtains pulled shut, it wasn't completely dark; a warm pink evening light sneaked through the fabric, bathing the room in a rosy glow. Molly lay in her bed listening to the sound of the ocean. If she kept very still, she could just about hear the faint lapping of the water as it surged up the beach, and was then sucked back by the force of the tide.

She reached out and took hold of her conch shell, wrapping her fingers around its smooth, cool surface. "Please, please take me to the mermaids tonight," she whispered, holding it tightly. "I think they need me."

She closed her eyes and lay listening to the sea. *Ssshhhh… Sssshhhhh… Sssshhhh…* went the waves as they rolled in and out.

And then, without any warning, Molly felt as if she were falling very fast from a great height. She could hear a rushing sound in her ears as she fell further and further, faster and faster…

"Molly… Molly… Molly…" called a voice, very faint, as if someone was shouting to her from far away.

Molly felt tingles all over as the falling sensation stopped, and she opened her eyes at last. She was on the seabed, with warm, azure water around her. Molly gasped in excitement and immediately gazed down at herself. Yes! She was wearing a turquoise top with her conch necklace around her throat, and where her legs had been, there now swung a sparkling green-scaled tail. She was a secret mermaid again – the shell's magic had worked!

Chapter Two

"Molly… Molly…" The voice came again – louder this time. Molly swung around to see one of the Shell-Keeper mermaids swimming toward her. It was Coral, smiling and waving, her dark hair streaming behind her and her violet eyes bright and welcoming. "Molly!" she cried, greeting her with a hug. "Oh, I'm so happy to see you."

Molly hugged her back. "I'm glad to be

here," she said – and then saw over Coral's shoulder where she was. "Oh," she said. "We're in the coral reef!"

Coral nodded, and the smile vanished from her face. "Yes," she said, "and doesn't it look awful?" She flung an arm out, pointing around them.

"Look – parts of the reef have become bleached, do you see?

All the algae have gone, and without them the
reef doesn't have enough energy to feed all the
creatures that come here."

Molly gazed around. The coral structures
of the reef were skeletal and white, and
looked rather eerie, looming through
the sea like ghostly fingers in every
direction. The whole place
seemed deserted.

"It wasn't so long ago that this reef was teeming with life," Coral went on miserably. "There were all kinds of colorful fish – clownfish, rays and pufferfish – plus there were sand sharks, sea cows, eels, squid, sea turtles…" Her voice trailed away. "And now they've all left to find new homes – if they can. Oh, if only I had my piece of the conch! I could work some healing magic to bring this reef back to life. But I still haven't found it – and I've been looking for days now!"

"I'll help you look," Molly said, wanting to comfort her. Coral gave a weak smile. "Thank you," she said. "I heard from the other Shell-Keepers that you've been amazing at helping them."

Molly blushed with pride. She knew that Carlotta, the bad mermaid queen, had originally stolen the five magical conch pieces from the Shell-Keeper mermaids, and taken them back to her dark cave. But when Molly first entered the Undersea Kingdom, the magic of Molly's sixth piccc of the conch had sent the shell pieces scattering through the ocean. With Molly's help,

Ella and Delphi had already found their pieces of the magical conch. Molly really hoped she could help Coral find hers too, in time to save the reef from dying out completely.

She felt a swishing sensation behind her just then and turned to see an enormous sea turtle gliding serenely through the water toward the two mermaids. "Oh!" Molly cried, delighted at the sight of such a huge, graceful creature. "Hello there."

The sea turtle had dark beady eyes
and a wide, friendly smile, but she looked
concerned. She sailed right up to Molly and
Coral, her flipper-like legs moving strongly
through the water. Her green shell was large
and heart-shaped, with yellowy edging.
"Hello," she said in a low, musical voice.
"Have you seen my baby? I can't find him
anywhere – the reef seems deserted."

Coral shook her head. "No, I haven't seen any creatures in this part of the reef for a while," she said, with rather a sad sigh. "I don't know where they've all gone."

The sea turtle gave a slow blink. "The sea horses say that there's one area of the reef that's still healthy – Tropical Valley, they're calling it," she replied. "And you know what the sea horses are like – they seem to hear everything first! So that's where I'm headed, just as soon as I can find my little one. He's still very small, and doesn't have a good sense of direction. I'm worried he's gotten lost, or stuck somewhere."

Molly bent to stroke the old turtle's head. "We'll look out for him," she promised. "I'm sure he can't have gone too far."

"Thank you," the turtle said. She waved goodbye with her flipper, and swam slowly away.

Molly and Coral watched her disappear into the damaged reef. "Maybe we should head for Tropical Valley too," Coral suggested thoughtfully. "If the reef is healthy there, it may mean my shell is somewhere close by." She shrugged. "You never know, some of the magic might have leaked out and be helping to protect that part of the reef."

Molly nodded. "We should definitely take a look," she said. "And if all the other creatures have taken refuge there, you could ask if any of them have seen your shell."

She and Coral swam away from the silent, empty reef, and Molly felt a shiver of relief as they left it behind. There was something very sad about being there – it felt as if they'd been standing in the ruins of an old house, hollow and lifeless, with nothing but ghosts and memories around them.

She gave herself a little shake. There was no point getting miserable and downcast about it – she and Coral had work to do. If they could find Coral's piece of conch shell, they would be able to help the reef flourish once more, and…

Molly was jerked out of her thoughts by a sudden scream. She glanced around to see Coral being dragged away from her by a strong whirling current. "Come back!" she yelled, without thinking, striking out after her friend. But seconds later, she regretted it.

For now, she was being pulled along by the mighty torrent of water too – and however hard Molly battled against it, she was powerless to swim in any other direction.

Chapter Three

It felt as if she were fighting the water, scrabbling at it with her arms, thrashing at it with her tail…but to no end. Nothing she did made any difference – she was trapped in the rushing current with Coral as it threw them roughly along. Was this something to do with the Dark Queen? She had tried to stop the Shell-Keepers from finding their conch pieces before.

"Use your shell," Coral cried out, trying to grab Molly's hand. "Quick, Molly!"

Of course! Molly had forgotten her shell in her fright at being swept away. Its magic had already helped her many times before. She glanced down, suddenly fearful that it might

have been tugged from its chain by the power
of the water, but it was still fastened around
her neck, swinging wildly. She clutched it,
dimly aware of a huge rock that loomed ahead
of them. If she and Coral were smashed against
it, then...

No time to think about that. The shell
suddenly felt hot beneath her fingers, as if
urging her to take action, and she shouted at the
top of her voice: "Conch, stop this current!"

Nothing happened for a second and Molly
felt another wave of sick fear sweep through her.
Oh no! Her command hadn't made any
difference – so now what? She and Coral were
tumbling closer and closer to the huge rock
ahead. Any second now they would be dashed
against it...she could almost imagine how the
hard rock would feel against her bare skin...

Molly tried again. "Conch, help us get out

of here!" she shouted desperately…and then the
magic seemed to work at last, and she and
Coral were tugged sharply out of the current as
if by an invisible hand. Suddenly they found
themselves in calmer waters, with millions of
tiny golden sparkles fizzling around their bodies,
while just a few yards away, the current
continued to hurtle along.

Molly felt shaky with relief. "Th-that was close," she stammered thankfully, her heart thudding. Her arms felt like jelly, weak and useless, after the pummeling they'd just taken from the water.

"That was terrifying," Coral agreed, her face pale as she gazed at the rock which stood just yards away from them. She pushed her dark hair off her face. "I've never known such a wild current. The ocean really is in trouble at the moment. Horrible Carlotta! She doesn't even care what danger she's caused by stealing our shells!"

"Which is why we've got to find your piece of the conch – and fast," Molly said. "Let's keep heading toward Tropical Valley. The sooner we get there, the better. Which way now?"

Coral hesitated. "I'm not sure," she said after a few moments. "I lost my bearings when the current dragged us off course like that. Let's see…"

The two mermaids stared around them, hoping to spot a landmark that they recognized. There was the huge rock right in front of them, looming like an enormous giant, Molly thought. Behind them, the way they'd just come, there stretched flat sand, with not a single creature in sight. To their left grew a vast forest of seaweed, dark and murky. "Thank goodness the current didn't drag us in there," Coral said, eyeing it with a shudder. "We'd never have found our way out!" On their right was a large tangled reef, whose tall twisted coral structures rose high in the water.

"I don't recognize this reef, but let's try going across it," Coral said, shrugging. "Hopefully I'll get my bearings and we'll be able to find Tropical Valley."

The two mermaids began making their way over the reef. It was quiet and empty, and whole patches of it were bare. Molly loved being a mermaid and exploring new parts of the ocean, but this reef seemed so desolate and unwell that it just made her sad to be there. It was so different from the vibrant picture in her spotter book.

Just as Molly was starting to feel as if they were the only living creatures in the ocean, Coral let out an excited shout.

"Look!" she cried.
"Over there, look!"

Molly followed Coral's pointing finger to see a cluster of ruby-red anemones blooming on a twist of coral

nearby; the first patch of color the mermaids had seen in the entire reef so far. Coral was smiling in delight. "This part of the reef is still alive!" she said happily.

"Oh, and look!" Molly said, suddenly spotting movement from the corner of her eye. A school of turquoise fish was swimming through the coral over on the right, their fins like bright little flags. And further ahead there was a rust-brown octopus, its long rubbery legs exploring a craggy section of rock.

Molly had never been so excited at the sight of sea creatures in her life. "This must be Tropical Valley – we're here!" she cried.

Chapter Four

"Fantastic," whooped Coral. A procession of little sea horses bobbed by just then, their tails curling below them as they swam.

Molly smiled at the sight. They were so cute, with their faces like miniature dragons. "Coral – look," she said, pointing them out. "Didn't the turtle say the sea horses know everything? Let's ask them if they've seen your shell anywhere!"

"Brilliant idea," Coral replied and called over to the sea horses. "Oh, excuse me, please!" She then launched into a series of clicking sounds to which the sea horses stopped and listened carefully.

The largest sea horse, who was coppery-brown with spines down his back, replied to Coral with similar clicking noises. He seemed quite excited about something, and two other sea horses joined in.

After the sea horses had sailed off in their
line again, Coral seized Molly's hands
and spun her around. "You were right," she
said. "I asked the sea horses if they'd seen
anything unusual in Tropical Valley...and
they said yes. Apparently, there's something
sparkly further ahead
in the reef. I think it
might be my shell!"

She laughed and a stream of silvery bubbles floated out of her mouth. Then she surged through the water, pulling Molly with her. "Let's go and find out!"

Coral's excitement was contagious. Molly's heart quickened as she swam after her friend over the teeming reef. And oh, there were so many amazing things to look at as they went! She saw eels slithering between plants and rocks, scuttling pink lobsters, and a whole rainbow of colorful fish. As for the reef itself…it was just beautiful. It was like swimming over a garden of bright flowers, all different shapes and colors.

"There's so much to see," Molly marveled. The sights were so amazing that she almost wanted to slow down and look at everything closely. She remembered her gran's words – a rainforest under the sea. She agreed. It was like nothing she'd ever seen before!

Coral didn't look quite so joyful. "There *is* a lot to see – and that could actually become a problem," she said. "Now that this is the only healthy area of the reef, it's almost bursting with sea creatures. There won't be enough food for all of them, so they won't all survive here. We've just *got* to get my conch to help bring the rest of the reef back to life!"

Molly fell silent and pushed herself forward even faster. Coral was right: this was no time to stop. They had to find her piece of conch as soon as possible.

It wasn't long before Coral let out a gasp. "Look – there's something shining ahead!" she cried, pointing.

Molly could see a trail of golden sparkles glittering in the water.

She and Coral swam quickly toward the light.
"My shell – it *is* my shell!" Coral cried joyfully
as they approached it. They could just see a
creamy-pink edge of the conch piece sticking
out from a hollow dip of coral, with more
golden sparkles shining out all around.

But just before they reached it, the two
mermaids heard a plaintive high-pitched
squeaking. "Somebody's crying for help," Coral
said. She stopped swimming and gazed around.

"There," Molly said, spotting a tiny baby
turtle who was stuck in a tangle of coral. Its little
green head was straining from side to side, and
its flippers were churning the water wildly, but
its shell had become wedged tight where it had
tried to swim through a narrow gap in the reef.

"Oh dear!" Coral exclaimed. "Poor little
one. Do you want some help?"

"I'm stuck!" the tiny creature wailed.

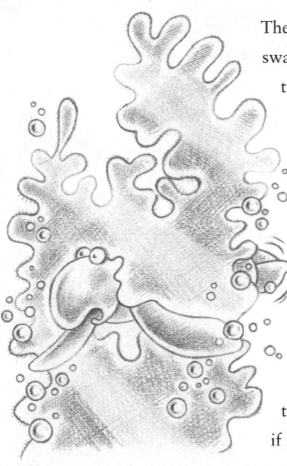

The two mermaids swam over to try to ease the baby turtle out, but it seemed quite firmly jammed in. "How long have you been trapped here?" Coral asked.

The baby turtle looked as if it were about to cry. "Ages," he said miserably. "I lost my mom and came here with my cousins – and now I've lost *them*, too. And then I got stuck!"

Something dawned on Molly. "I think
we might have seen your mom!" she said
excitedly, remembering the giant green turtle.
"She was looking for you – she's still back
at the old reef."

The baby turtle hung his head and his
mouth trembled. "She'll never find me now,
then!" he said. "I should have waited for her
before I left with the others. I thought she must
have gone ahead."

Coral stroked him soothingly. "Don't worry," she said. "We'll get you out. Then, as soon as I've grabbed my shell, we'll help find your mom, won't we, Molly?"

But Molly wasn't listening. She'd just seen something scary approaching. A whole swarm of jellyfish was heading straight for Coral's shell, their bodies glowing a strange red in the water.

"Coral, look!" she cried in alarm.

Coral stared – and a look of horror crossed her face. "Oh no! They must be from the Dark Queen," she said. "And they're poisonous too. You must stay away from their tentacles, Molly. They have a nasty sting." She clapped a hand over her mouth. "What are we going to do?"

Chapter Five

Molly felt scared as more and more jellyfish drifted menacingly toward where Coral's conch piece was glittering. They were so many of them, with their dangling tentacles and that sinister red glow – very different than the pale moon jellyfish she'd found in Horseshoe Bay earlier. "Should we be brave and try to storm through them?" she asked, even though she wasn't feeling very brave at all.

She shuddered at the thought of their soft deadly tentacles on her skin.

Coral shook her head. "No way," she said. "If they sting you with their venom, you'll be in big trouble." She groaned. "I can't believe it! Why didn't I just grab my conch while I had the chance?"

"We've got to get them away from it," Molly said, thinking hard. "Maybe if we distract them somehow…"

Coral nodded. "Yes – if we can lure them away, I could dart across and grab my shell. But how?"

Molly took a deep breath. "Maybe I can tempt some of them away with *my* shell," she suggested. "I'm sure the Dark Queen would love to get her hands on it, wouldn't she? If I show it to them, they might come after me first – leaving your shell for you to get."

Coral looked doubtful. "Molly, I'm not

sure," she said. "They are very dangerous.
I know you can swim fast, but…"

Molly knew that she had to try. "Coral,
it's the only thing I can think of. And
I'll ask my shell for help if I get
stuck. I know it's
not powerful
enough to get
rid of all the
jellyfish, but
it should protect
me. You stay hidden,
and get your conch
when the coast is clear."

Coral hugged her.
"You are so brave,"
she said. "If
you're really sure,
then… Good luck."

"Good luck!" the baby turtle chimed in. His dark beady eyes looked fearful.

"Thanks," Molly said. She patted the turtle gently. "We'll be back to help you very soon," she said. Then she swam quickly away from Coral so that her friend couldn't see the nervous expression on her face. She felt absolutely terrified!

She swam a little closer to the jellyfish, her heart racing. They were clustered over Coral's shell now, and the biggest few had wrapped their floaty tentacles protectively around it and were trying to heave it up from its resting place.

Molly really didn't like the look of them.
She had already met several creatures enslaved
by Carlotta's dark magic and each encounter
had been very scary. She was sure the jellyfish
would be quick to attack her if they thought she
was going to stop them from taking Coral's
piece of conch. Her fingers trembled on her
shell. She'd just have to hope she could get

away faster than they could
chase her.

"Hey, over here!"
she called to them.
Her voice shook a
little on the words
as she saw the
mass of jellyfish
shift at her shout.
"Look what I've
got!" she yelled,

clutching her conch piece. "Mine's much better than that one, don't you think?"

Her heart pounded even faster and adrenalin coursed through her, as she braced herself for the fastest swim of her life. Were they going to turn on her, try to grab her shell with those venomous ribbony tentacles? Would they wrap themselves around her arms and neck, stinging her with their poison until she was weak and limp?

A few of them broke away from the group and drifted closer to her, but they didn't seem interested enough. After a moment or two, they merely floated back to help the others pick up Coral's shell. Maybe the Dark Queen had given them strict orders to get Coral's piece of the conch, and that alone, Molly thought, feeling her spirits sinking. Whatever the reason, they weren't budging.

So now what should she do? How could she get them to move away?

She held her shell and it glowed softly through her fingers – and as it did so, she saw a similar pink light sparkling around Coral's shell. Then she remembered how the last time she'd been in the ocean with another mermaid, Delphi, they had been able to create very strong magic when they put their shells together. Of course, it would be impossible for Molly to swim over to Coral's shell with her own – the jellyfish would be sure to sting or attack her – but maybe there was another way...

She swam quickly over to Coral and voiced her thoughts. "We need to get my shell piece to touch yours somehow – I think their combined magic could get rid of the jellyfish! Maybe if I put my necklace on a length of seaweed, and threw it toward your shell?" she suggested.

"That way I could tug it back and try again if I miss."

Coral bit her lip. "It's very risky," she said. "What if the seaweed broke? I couldn't bear it if we lost your shell too, Molly. We wouldn't be able to get it back while the jellyfish were near it. Isn't there any other way?"

There was silence for a moment, then a small voice piped up. "*I* could take it. Molly's piece of the conch, I mean. The jellyfish can't harm me, with my hard shell."

Molly had almost forgotten about the little turtle, and gazed at him in surprise. "Do you mean it?" she asked. "Would you really do that for us?"

The turtle grinned. "Sure!" he said. He tapped a flipper against the coral that enclosed him. "That's if you can get me out of here, of course."

Coral smiled. "There's something we haven't tried," she said. "Molly, maybe touching your conch piece to the reef would help."

Molly did so at once. "Conch, please free the turtle," she said. At her words, her shell suddenly shone with a silvery-white light...and then the coral structure bent outwards as if it were made of rubber so that the turtle could easily swim through it.

"Thank you, thank you!" squeaked the baby turtle, swimming around in small circles. Then he butted his head playfully against Molly's arm. "Now...why don't you tie that necklace around my middle, and I'll see what I can do."

Molly undid her necklace with trembling fingers and secured it around the turtle so that the shell dangled from his belly. She really didn't like the thought of her magical conch piece being away from her, but this was the best chance they had.

"Please look after it," she begged him. "Please don't let them get it."

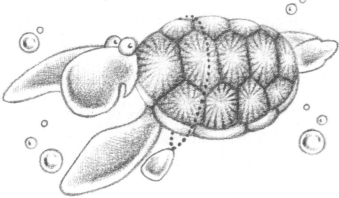

"I'll do my best," he assured her, and off he went.

Molly and Coral swam a safe distance behind him. He was so tiny and young, Molly wasn't at all sure that this plan would work. What if the jellyfish pushed him away – or dragged her necklace off him? Her mouth felt dry with fear at the thought of having to swim over and fight for her conch piece. But…wait… what was happening now?

The turtle had reached the first of the jellyfish and began to barge through them, seemingly with no trouble at all – but Molly still held her breath. Then she stared in surprise as the two conch pieces began glowing brighter and brighter the closer together they came. "Something is happening," Coral murmured, gripping Molly's hand. For a moment they lost sight of the turtle as he disappeared into the densest part of the jellyfish swarm. When they finally caught a glimpse of him again, he was very close to Coral's shell – and then suddenly he was close enough that the two conch pieces touched one another! There was a dazzling flash of light and the water crackled with white sparkles.

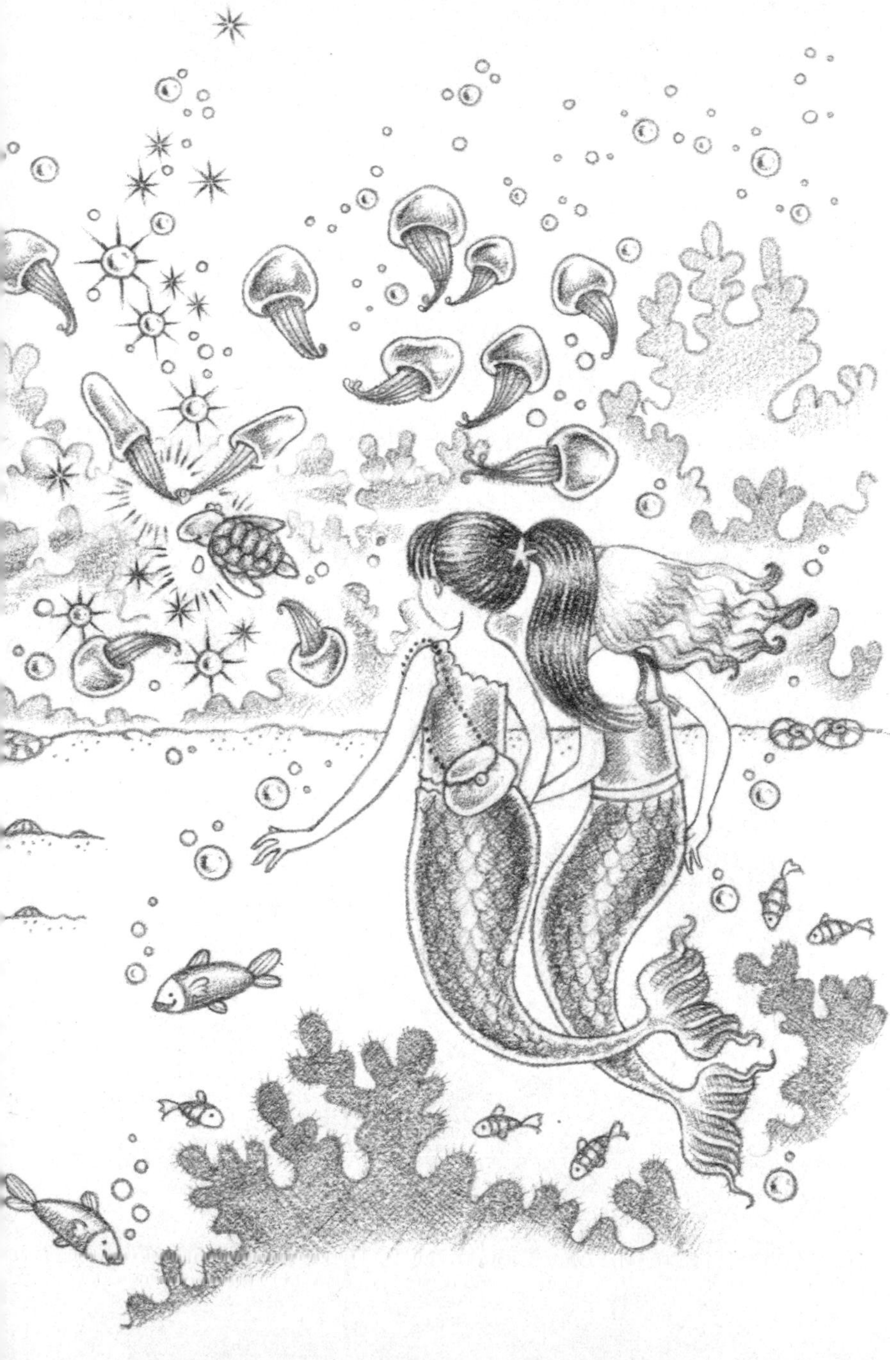

Whoosh! The jellyfish seemed to bounce off Coral's shell, as if thrown away by a powerful force. "Yes!" cheered Molly. The clever turtle had done it! She and Coral sped forward to touch their shells. "Conch, send the jellyfish away!" Coral shouted at the top of her voice.

Molly watched in astonishment as a great surge of water came from nowhere...and

pushed the mass of jellyfish away. Off they went, tumbling helplessly together, turning somersaults, their tentacles becoming tangled. The plan had actually worked!

"Whoopee!" the turtle squeaked, waving its flippers up and down.

Coral, who was grinning from ear to ear, showered kisses on the brave little creature.

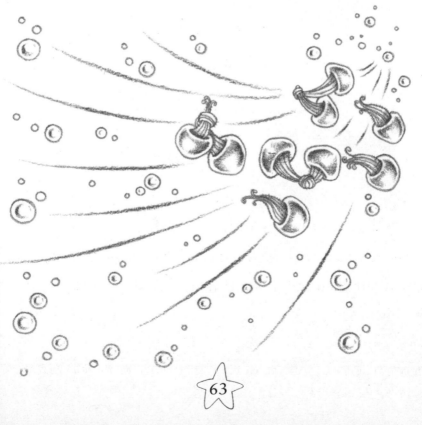

"Well done, oh, well done!" she cried, gently untying Molly's necklace and handing it back to her. She clutched her own shell in triumph.

"Oh, I'm so happy to have this back! Molly, that was amazing, wasn't it? The way the force of our shell-magic sent them shooting away, like a…"

Molly had stopped listening, though. She was staring through the rushing water, trying to see past the whirling jellyfish in the distance. What was that? Or rather, *who* was that? She was sure she'd just spotted a dark-haired mermaid almost getting caught up in the wave of jellyfish. She couldn't be certain but for a second, the mermaid had looked very much like Princess Silva, the Merqueen's daughter!

Chapter Six

"And now I can begin healing the reef," Coral was saying behind her, "and repairing some of the damage. Queen Luna will be so delighted."

By now, the mysterious mermaid had vanished. Confused, Molly turned back to Coral. "That's strange. I think I just saw Princess Silva," she said nervously. "I hope she's all right – it looked like she almost got swept away with the jellyfish."

Coral looked puzzled. "Princess Silva? Are you sure? No – she wouldn't be all the way out here." A thought struck her and her eyes widened. "Did the mermaid have a big hooked nose and a black cape?" she asked. "It might have been Carlotta!"

Molly shook her head, remembering the pale young mermaid she'd seen clinging onto the reef. "No – the mermaid I saw was pretty," she replied. "I think, anyway," she added, starting to doubt herself. "Maybe I was wrong."

"I'm sure it wasn't the princess," Coral said confidently. "Honestly, Molly, I've never seen her out here before. We're a long way from the palace. Anyway, whoever it was, I'm sure she's fine. She'd have called for help otherwise, wouldn't she?" She put her hands on her hips and smiled at the turtle. "Now then, we've got a turtle to take back to his mom, don't we?"

"Yes, yes!" squeaked the turtle.

Coral opened the pale purple bag that she wore around her shoulder and popped her shell carefully inside. "Room for one more!" she said, holding it open for the turtle. "Go on, jump in. I'll give you a ride."

The baby turtle was very excited and swam inside the bag at once. He did look sweet, with just his head poking out of the top!

"Ready? Then let's go," Coral said. And off they swam.

Coral's shell really was amazing, Molly thought, as they left Tropical Valley behind and swam across the bleached, empty reef. Sparks kept shooting out of Coral's purple bag, and the water seemed to fizz with healing light. "Oooh," the baby turtle kept giggling from where he was nestled in the bag. "That tickles!"

Coral smiled. "It won't be long before this reef is *all* healthy," she told Molly. "My shell is already sending its healing powers far and wide.

In a few weeks, the creatures will have plenty of places to make their homes. They won't all have to stay in Tropical Valley."

The baby turtle stopped giggling suddenly and let out an excited squeak. "Mommy! There's my mommy!" He squirmed and wiggled his way out of Coral's bag, and zipped into the water, his flippers flailing as he propelled himself toward a large green turtle in the distance.

Coral and Molly watched as the mother turtle turned and saw her baby. And yes, it *was* the same turtle they'd seen earlier. "There you are!" the mother cried, throwing her big flippers around her baby in a hug. Her dark eyes shut

in happiness as she held him close. "I was so worried about you!"

"The mermaids helped me," the baby turtle said, snuggling into her.

"And *he* helped *us*," Molly said. "He was amazing!"

71

The mother turtle turned and smiled gratefully at the mermaids. "Thank you for finding him," she said. "Now we can go to Tropical Valley with everyone else."

Coral took her shell from its bag. "Well... you know, you might want to stay here, after all," she said. She pressed her conch shell against the bleached coral and muttered a few magical-sounding words. There was a flash of light all around them – so bright Molly had to close her eyes. And when she opened them...

"Wow!" she cried. "How did that just happen?" It was like being in a different place. The reef was already beginning to glow with colors – faint at first, but becoming stronger and brighter by the second. Plants were starting to bloom from crevices in the rocks, opening as Molly watched.

Coral grinned. "Oh, it's good to have my shell back!" she cried, planting a big kiss on her conch piece.

The mother turtle looked delighted. "We *will* go to Tropical Valley," she said decisively, "but only to tell the others the great news. They can all come home again. Thank you!"

Coral bobbed a little curtsy. "My pleasure," she said. "I'll come and visit you soon. Goodbye!"

After saying goodbye to the turtles, Molly and Coral struck out again for the Undersea Kingdom. They left the reef behind and swam for some time through clear waters, until Molly saw the familiar golden gates that marked the entrance to the kingdom.

It felt wonderful to swim through the gates, knowing that Coral's shell was safely back with its keeper. Other mermaids stopped what they were doing and nudged each other at Coral's return. "Have you got it? Have you got your shell?" they called out eagerly.

Coral held up her bag and grinned at them. "We got it!" she replied happily.

With all the cheering and clapping that greeted this announcement, Molly felt as if she and Coral were famous. Several mermaids darted ahead to the Merqueen's palace. "Queen Luna, Queen Luna!" they called excitedly. "Wonderful news, Your Majesty!"

The queen's head appeared through one of the palace windows at the sound of their voices. Her eyes brightened at the sight of Coral and Molly approaching, and then a wide grin stretched across her face.

"Coral, Molly! You're back!" she cried, swimming out of a nearby doorway toward them. "And so is my piece of the magical conch," Coral cried, the words bubbling out of her joyfully. "Carlotta sent an army of jellyfish to try to stop us, but Molly and a brave little turtle helped to send them away."

Molly felt her cheeks turn pink as the queen bestowed a dazzling smile upon her. "Oh, my secret mermaid, it is good to have you on our side," Queen Luna said, taking Molly's hands in hers. "Thank you – again!"

Molly bobbed a curtsy, blushing even deeper with pride. "I'm glad I could help," she said. And then she remembered the dark-haired mermaid she thought she had seen. "But...we might have caused something awful to happen too."

Chapter Seven

Coral put an arm around her. "Have you been worrying about that this whole time?" she asked in surprise. "I'm sure she's fine. And it couldn't really have been the princess."

The Merqueen raised her eyebrows. "The princess? What do you mean?"

Haltingly, Molly told the Merqueen what she thought she'd seen, her feelings of triumph fading as she spoke. Coral was probably right, she'd no doubt gotten it wrong, but all the same…she felt nervous. What if it *had* been Princess Silva out there near all the jellyfish? Oh, why hadn't they stopped to check?

"How odd," Queen Luna said once Molly had finished. "I don't think it could have been the princess, though. I'm sure she's been here all afternoon. Let's take a look on the Seeing Stone to make sure."

Molly and Coral followed the Merqueen through the palace and out to the courtyard where Molly had first met all her fellow Shell-Keeper mermaids. There was the large white rock, which could show the Merqueen what was happening all over her kingdom and even in some other parts of the ocean. "Silva," Queen Luna said simply and pressed her hands to it for a moment. Molly found that she was holding her breath as the image appeared.

Then her breath rushed out in relief as she saw the princess sitting in her bedchamber, making a tiara from white pieces of shell.

"There," Queen Luna said. "She's perfectly okay. Nothing to worry about. Still, we should make absolutely sure the mermaid you saw is all right." She called to one of her assistants. "Send out a rescue party to a reef known as Tropical Valley, please," she instructed. "There may be a mermaid in distress who needs help."

Off went the assistant immediately…and then, to Molly's dismay, the queen glanced upwards at a shaft of light that was beaming down through the water. Molly's heart sank. She knew what that meant by now – her adventure was over, and it was time to return home!

The queen caught the doleful expression on Molly's face and hugged her. "You'll be back soon, I hope," she said. "We still have two more pieces of the conch to find, after all – and we need you to help us."

Molly managed a smile. "Of course I'll help," she said. "I'll always help as much as I can."

Coral hugged Molly too. "Thank you," she said. "I couldn't have done it without you."

Molly had a lump in her throat as she said goodbye.

She hated leaving
the mermaid world
behind! But the
water was whirling
all around her
suddenly, spinning
her so fast that
she could no
longer see her
friends. She felt
as if she was rising
up, up, higher
and higher...

And then she was opening her eyes, in her own bed at home. Sun was sliding into her room under the bottoms of the curtains, and she could hear the sea out in the bay, the waves rushing up the beach.

She sat up – and realized there was something in her hand. She opened her fingers to see a pure-white shell, tall and twisted like a whipped ice cream, with an opening at one end.

It was cool and smooth, shining white on her palm in the morning sun. Maybe it had once lain on the seabed under the reef? She smiled, thinking happily of the coral reefs growing back strongly now, thanks to the healing magic of Coral's conch.

She got out of bed, still holding her shell. "I wonder if this is in my spotter book?" she said to herself, and swung her legs out of bed.

There was a whole page of seaside shells to spot – and she'd certainly never seen one as pretty as this before.

She smiled again, thinking about all the amazing creatures she'd seen on her mermaid adventures now – enough to fill an entire spotter book all by themselves!

She skipped down for breakfast feeling very happy as she wondered what she might see on her *next* secret mermaid adventure...

The End

The Secret Mermaid

For more magical
underwater adventures visit
www.edcpub.com
or
www.usbornebooksandmore.com

To find out more
about Molly and all her
mermaid friends, and have
some magical ocean fun,
check out

www.secret-mermaid.com

Sue Mongredien has published over 60 books, including the magical *Oliver Moon, Junior Wizard* series. Like Molly Holmes, Sue loves exploring, and gave up a job as an editor of children's books to travel the world, before becoming a full-time writer. Sue also loves the sea, and had a house near Brighton beach in England before moving to Bath, also in England, where she now lives with her husband and three children.

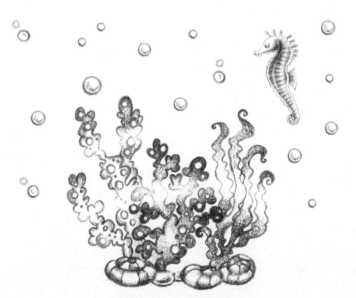

If you've enjoyed **The Secret Mermaid**,
you might also enjoy:

Amy Wild, Animal Talker

by Diana Kimpton

Welcome to the world of Amy Wild, where
dogs tell their secrets, cats perform rescue
missions, and an entire island is squeaking
and squawking with animal magic!

Animal lovers everywhere will be
instantly enchanted by this Dr. Dolittle
for a new generation.

The Pony-Crazed Princess

by Diana Kimpton

Princess Ellie is crazy about horses!
And she's fed up with being a princess!
She hates frilly pink dresses, and boring
waving lessons. She'd much rather be
riding one of her four gorgeous ponies!

SUNDANCE

RAINBOW

SHADOW

MOONBEAM